STEVE

A story about death

by

Marjorie Newman

W
FRANKLIN WATTS
NEW YORK•LONDON•SYDNEY

First published in 1995 by Franklin Watts

This paperback edition published in 1998

Franklin Watts
96 Leonard Street
London EC2A 4RH

Franklin Watts Australia
14 Mars Road
Lane Cove
NSW 2066

Editor: Rosemary McCornick
Designer: Jason Anscomb
A CIP catalogue record for this book
is available from the British Library

ISBN 0 7496 3284 4 (pbk)
       0 7496 2026 9 (hbk)

Dewey Classification 306.9

Printed in Great Britain

Foreword

Dying is a very frightening thought for many of us. Living is so much easier to discuss, and think about.

Death comes in many ways: accidentally; through short or long term illness; naturally from old age; even at birth. No one ever reacts to death in an identical manner. We all respond to news of death differently.

For some there will be a sense of relief. This can often happen when someone close has been ill and the pain of watching life slowly slip away has been almost too much to bear. For others there will be shock, disbelief or denial, especially if death is the result of a tragic accident.

All or most people will experience varying degrees of sorrow. Feelings of anger are not unusual if the parting was swift and unexpected and did not allow for "good-byes". There may be tremendous pain if the departed loved one was taken from the family in childhood. This pain is often accompanied by utter confusion about life and reasons for living.

Fortunately, family, friends and time are great healers. After the darkness of grief, there will come a time when pleasant memories replace sad ones. Then thoughts of the loved and lost person will become happy recollections of special times together. And, having survived the loss of a loved friend or family member, there is often a stronger determination and ability to face the future. Memories of precious smiles and treasured conversations remain for ever. And these memories are never more than a thought away.

Dot Grace
Education Welfare South West Division, Hampshire County Council

One

Steve looked at the clock on the classroom wall. Ten minutes to home time. He couldn't wait for school to be over. He wanted to get back to his new metal detector. To try it out in the garden before Dad came home. Maybe he'd find some treasure right away. That would be great! He'd take it to his Junior Metal Detecting Club. Probably the only such club in the whole country . . .

A boy came into the room and whispered to the teacher. Mr Blenkinsop looked at Steve.

"Steven Martin! The headmaster wants you. In his room."

Everyone turned round. Steve knew what they were thinking. He must be in trouble. He couldn't be. He hadn't done anything. Nothing that Mr Grimes could know about anyway.

"Mr Grimes would like it to be today, Steven. If you can manage it," said Mr Blenkinsop.

Steve blushed. He scraped back his chair and hurried out of the room. His heart beat fast as he went along the corridor.

When he reached the headmaster's room he was amazed to see his sister, Gemma, there. Sitting down! She looked up at him, questioning. Steve shook his head.

"Come in, Steven." Mr Grimes spoke kindly. "Sit down, lad. I have to tell you something."

So they weren't in trouble. Steve sat. Mr Grimes cleared his throat.

"Your mother can't come to meet you tonight," he began.

"Why not?" cried Gemma. Nine years old and she still hasn't learned when to keep quiet, thought Steve. Sisters two years younger than yourself could be a pain. He was surprised Mr Grimes didn't tell her off for interrupting.

"She's asked Mrs Vickers to meet you, instead," Mr Grimes went on. He hasn't answered Gemma, thought Steve. A cold feeling began to spread over him. Something was wrong.

"But -" Gemma began. Mr Grimes continued.

"Your father had an accident at work this afternoon. He's been taken to hospital. Your mother has gone too, to find out what's going on. She'll be home as soon as possible."

"But Dad works in an office," said Steve.

"How could he have had an accident?" Gemma's voice sounded rude. "He's the boss. Martin and Company." Again Mr Grimes didn't tell her off.

"Your father was visiting a demolition site," he explained. "A wall fell on him."

"Like on television sometimes?" asked Gemma. Mr Grimes nodded. "Your mother will be able to tell you more later," he said.

The bell rang for home time. Gemma sprang up. Steve stood up more slowly. He felt very cold.

"See you tomorrow then," said Mr Grimes. "Remember, if Mrs Vickers isn't outside, come back to me."

But Mrs Vickers was outside. Her car was crowded with children and animals as usual.

"I want to go and see Dad at the hospital!" announced Gemma from the pavement.

"Can we?" Steve asked eagerly.

Mrs Vickers pushed the hair back from her hot face.

"Better come home with me and have some tea, pets," she said. "Your mum will expect you to be at my house. She'll ring the minute there's any news."

Steve could see it was no good. Anyway they could never go to the hospital with that carload.

"Come on, Gem," he said. "Aren't you hungry?" Gemma was always starving.

Today she hesitated for a minute. Then she said, "Yes."

"Good," approved Mrs Vickers. "Hop in."

They squashed into the back with the black labrador, Rover, the Scottie, Barney, two-year-old Thomas and four-year-old Mark. Five-year-old Rebecca was settled in the front seat and wouldn't give it up.

"She's in a mood," Mrs Vickers explained, driving erratically up the road and just missing the lollipop lady.

"Am not!" frowned Rebecca.

Rover leaned over the back of the seat and licked her ear. She giggled. That set Thomas off. Thomas's giggle made them all laugh. Steve felt a bit better. He lifted Barney on to his lap, and hugged him.

Mrs Vickers made scrambled eggs on toast for tea. Steve couldn't eat much. Even Gemma refused any cake to follow.

Mrs Vickers put the television on. Rover sat himself on the settee and had to be pushed off. Mark, Rebecca, Thomas and Gemma quickly took his place. The moment they were settled, Rover jumped up and sat on top of them, spreading himself along their laps. Thomas started to giggle again. Barney began to bark at a dog on the screen. Rebecca shouted at him to be quiet. Mark shouted at her to be quiet. Gemma put her fingers in her ears, and yelled louder than anyone. Steve looked at Mrs Vickers.

"Mayhem," she smiled. "It always is for the next half hour or so. They're letting off steam. Gemma too." Steve tried to smile. But the cold feeling was coming back. Why hadn't Mum rung?

TWO

Suddenly there was a knock at the front door. Mrs Vickers hurried to open it. Mum was on the doorstep. Uncle Bob was with her. Steve stood in the kitchen doorway, not moving.

"Margaret?" said Mrs Vickers. Then, "Margaret! Oh no!"

Gemma rushed out of the sitting room.

"Mum! Mum! What's happened? Where's Dad? Why didn't he come home with you?"

The other children and the dogs came out and milled around. Mrs Vickers shooed them all back into the sitting room and shut the door. Mum and Uncle Bob were in the hall now.

Gemma was clinging to Mum, shaking her to make her answer.

Mrs Vickers whispered, "Gemma, pet..."

"What?" said Steve. Then he shouted, "What?"

Gently Uncle Bob drew Gemma away from Mum.

"Gemma, Steve, it's sad news, I'm afraid. When the wall fell on your dad it knocked him out. He never came round."

"What d'you mean?" Steve could hear himself shouting. "Mum?"

Mum managed to speak. "He died, darling. Just now. At the hospital."

Gemma shook herself free from Uncle Bob. She was furious, stamping her foot.

"It's not true! He didn't die. Why won't you let me go and see him?"

It was a nightmare. Steve felt sick.

Mrs Vickers was very kind. She made them all sit down in her kitchen and gave them cups of hot, strong tea with plenty of sugar. She said they could stay for as long as they wanted. Then she went into the sitting room to hush her children.

Gemma sobbed as she drank. Twice she spluttered and nearly choked. Uncle Bob patted her on the back.

Mum was silent. Steve wanted her to talk, to make everything all right, the way she always did.

Only tonight she didn't.

Presently Uncle Bob took them back to their own house. As they went indoors, Mum started to cry. Gemma was frightened. She began to shout again, stamping, yelling.

Uncle Bob spoke sharply. "Gemma, stop that! At once!"

Gemma took a deep breath - and stopped. Mum sobbed, "I'll be all right in a minute," and rushed upstairs. Awkwardly, Steve put his arm round Gemma. She clung to him. She'd never done that before. He felt as if he must take care of her.

"Come on, you two." Uncle Bob took them into

the sitting room. He told them more of what had happened.

"The ambulance rushed your dad to hospital. The paramedics started work even on the way. The doctors and nurses were waiting. Everyone did everything they could. But it was no use. There's one good thing - your dad couldn't have known anything about it."

Gemma was quiet now. She looked sleepy. Uncle Bob didn't seem surprised. He switched on the television, then went upstairs to Mum.

Presently Mum and Uncle Bob came down. Mum sat on the settee. Steve curled up next to her. Gemma had dozed off in the armchair.

Uncle Bob had to go.

"See you tomorrow," he promised. He let himself out.

Mum and Steve sat together for what seemed like a long time. Neither of them wanted to talk. After a while Mum said, "We'd better get to bed. You and Gemma have school in the morning."

School? How could anyone go to school, after this?

Mum knew what he was thinking.

"Carrying on as usual is best," she said. "As much as we can."

They woke Gemma. They all tried to drink some hot milk. Then they went to bed.

Steve tossed and turned. He couldn't get comfortable. He sat up, switched on the light and tried

to read. Then he remembered his metal detector.
He got it out. Would it make too much noise if he had
a go now, indoors?

Suddenly he remembered he and Dad had been
going to try it out together. He threw the metal detector
on to the bed and rushed along the passage to Mum.
The bedroom light was on. Gemma was there already.
Mum held out her arms. The three of them cuddled
down under the bedclothes. It was morning when Steve
woke.

Three

School felt strange. The other children had heard about the accident. It had been on the television news.
Steve felt as if they were all staring at him. Why didn't they just carry on as usual? Why didn't they talk to him? Perhaps they didn't know what to say.

Gemma was talking. Talking about school things. Maybe she still didn't believe it had happened...

Mr Blenkinsop asked him and Gemma to sort some books instead of going in to Assembly. Steve guessed why.

Mr Grimes was going to talk about the accident. He didn't want them to have to listen.

Steve was glad when lessons started, even though he got everything wrong.

At playtime he stood by the wall.

"Hi!" His friend Jim was coming over, looking the same as usual.

"Hi," Steve answered.

"Want a sweet?"

"Thanks." The toffee looked as if it had been in Jim's pocket for months, but it tasted OK.

Jim unwrapped one for himself, put it in his mouth.

"You know our club?" he said.

"Metal detecting? Yes?" Steve was glad Jim was a member too. There were only ten members, all aged between nine and twelve.

"You know we're having that camp at Jukes' Farm at half term?"

"Wednesday, Thursday, Friday. Of course I know." Steve was puzzled.

"Are you still coming?"

Steve realised what Jim was getting at. Would it make a difference, now that Dad was dead?

"Sure I'm coming!" he declared.

But he wasn't sure. Could they afford it now? He was glad to get back into school.

The morning wore on. By lunch time Steve was hungry. School dinner tasted good. Steve had seconds. Then thirds.

After dinner he and Jim kicked a ball around, just as usual. Steve gave it a hard kick. It went soaring up and landed in Mrs Spriggs the dinner lady's huge handbag.

"Sorry!" gasped Steve.

"Go and play down the other end!" ordered Mrs Spriggs, getting the ball out for him.

Jim and Steve dashed away, giggling.

"Her face when she saw it land!" chuckled Jim.

"Wonder what she keeps in that bag," puffed Steve.

"Her nightie," suggested Jim. They doubled up at the picture in their minds.

"Treasure!" said Steve when they'd stopped laughing. "She could get a lot in there. When we're metal detecting we'll need a bag like that."

They were silent, dreaming of the hoards of coins and jewels they would find. Mr Soames, their club leader, had said Jukes' Farm was a very good site for metal detecting.

If I am allowed to go, Steve thought with a sudden shiver. Nothing was certain, the way it had been before.

But Mum was there at home time, as usual. That was nice...

Then suddenly, after tea, Gemma burst out, "Dad isn't dead! It's not true! He's still in the hospital in one of those intensive care wards! That's why we can't go and see him! One day he'll get better and come home again!"

Steve felt sick. Mum's face went very white.

"Darling Gemma, it is true. We have to face it. He won't be coming home any more. His body is in the chapel of rest, at the undertakers."
Gemma shook her head.

Mum asked quietly, "Would you both like to see where the accident happened? And then come with me to see Dad's body?"

Neither of them answered. Mum went on.

"Mr Watkins, at the site, said we could go any time. So did Mr Bradford at the undertakers."

"What - " Steve began. He wanted to say, "What

will Dad look like?" But he couldn't. "What is the chapel of rest like?" he asked instead.

Gemma was listening, looking stubborn.

"Mr Bradford's chapel of rest is a lovely room," Mum said. "I saw it today. It's decorated in blue. There are beautiful flowers and soft music. There are some candles too. In the middle of the room there's a long table. Dad's coffin is on the table. The coffin has a white silk lining. Dad's body is lying in the coffin. He's wearing a white shirt. His hands are folded over his chest. His skin looks whiter than usual, and there are some blue spots on it. His eyes are shut."

She looked at them both.

"Whatever you decide to do is all right," she said. "But I think it might help Gemma to go. There's nothing to be afraid of."

Gemma said, "I want to."

"To go to the building site?" asked Mum.

"And to the chapel of rest," said Gemma.

Steve swallowed hard. "I want to come with you," he decided.

"We'll go tomorrow after school," Mum promised. That night they all slept in Mum's bed again. It wasn't something they would do for ever. They just needed to be with her for now.

Steve woke in the morning feeling sick. He wondered if he should tell Mum he'd changed his mind.

He looked across the breakfast table at Gemma.

She looked miserable. It was no good. He couldn't let her go without him.

Four

School next day was hard. Steve's thoughts kept drifting away from work.

At home time Gemma was in Mum's car before him. She was in the front passenger seat.

"Why can't I ever sit in the front?" demanded Steve crossly.

"You do!" cried Gemma. "More than me!"

"That's not true! It's always you!" declared Steve. He hated her.

"You can have next turn, Steve," promised Mum. Steve climbed into the back. He didn't know why he felt so cross. He didn't know why he hated everyone just at that moment.

He couldn't keep it up. Hating Gemma. As soon as she saw where the wall had fallen on Dad she began to cry. It was the first time she'd really believed it. Mr Watkins took Gemma and Mum into the site office. Steve wandered around outside.

"Hullo there!"

Steve turned round. One of the workmen had come over. It was Frank. Dad had talked about him sometimes.

"Sorry about your dad, Steve." Frank looked awkward.

Steve didn't know how to answer. It was the first time anyone had said that to him when he was on his own.

A polite, "It's all right, thank you," came to his mind. But that would have been utterly stupid, because it wasn't all right. It wasn't all right.

Frank said, "I heard you're keen on metal detecting."

Steve looked at Frank with sudden interest.

"I do a bit of that myself," Frank said. "It gets you hooked, doesn't it! All that treasure lying about waiting to be discovered. Every time you go out you think, this could be it! The day I make my fortune!"

"Yes," Steve agreed. He always thought that.

"Have you found much?" he asked.

"A golden guinea's my best up till now," Frank answered, sounding careless.

"A golden guinea?" Steve's eyes shone.

"I found it at the edge of an old footpath," Frank grinned. He wasn't trying to hide his pride any longer.

"Then you could keep it!" Steve said.

"Right," nodded Frank. "I could tell you some tales about metal detecting!" he added. "Have you heard about finding sheep?"

Steve laughed.

"It's true!" Frank declared. "In Yorkshire, I think it was. There was this great snowstorm, and the sheep were still out in the fields - some of them buried in drifts. People were going frantic, giving them up for lost.

But the farmer remembers something. Those sheep were wearing tags on their ears. Metal tags."

"He didn't -"

"He did. Went out with his detector and found every one of them. Under the snow."

"Were they - ?"

"Dead? Not them. All saved," Frank replied heartily.

Steve breathed a sigh of relief.

"Steve!" Mum was calling him from the site-office door. Gemma had stopped crying and was hopping from one foot to the other, impatient to be gone.

"See you again maybe," said Frank.

"I hope so," Steve replied. He meant it.

Frank looked pleased.

This time Gemma actually got into the back seat of the car. Steve sat in front and thought about Frank all the way to the undertakers.

After all, it wasn't as hard as they'd expected. Seeing Dad. Somehow the real Dad wasn't there any more.

Steve squeezed Gemma's hand. She didn't squeeze back.

She was just very quiet.

Mum took them both to the fast-food place. They had hot dogs and milk shakes.

"Uncle Bob's coming round tomorrow," she said.

"He's taking us all to Seamouth for the day."

"In his car?" asked Steve.

"Of course his car," said Mum. "Ours would never make it!"

Steve grinned. Gemma announced, "I'm going to swim, and I don't care if it is a bit cold."

Mum's eyes met Steve's. Thank goodness she's feeling better, they agreed.

"Can I take my metal detector?" he asked.

"As long as you let me have a go!" said Mum.

"And me!" cried Gemma.

"All right. As long as I have first go," grinned Steve.

In the end they all had a go. Uncle Bob as well. They'd hoped to find a gold watch at least. But all they found were a few modern coins.

"Enough for a large ice cream for me!" claimed Uncle Bob, kneeling up on the sand. Steve and Gemma tackled him together. He rolled over under their weight.

"I give in!" he yelled. "Ice creams all round! My treat!"

They sat on the sea wall, licking their ice creams. The sun shone. People walked by, laughing and talking. Steve brushed his metal detector free of sand.

He had a sudden thought.

"Mum," he said, "will I still be able to go on the trip with my club?"

"Of course!" cried Mum and Uncle Bob together.

Steve was glad they'd had a good day, because the minister called that evening to talk about Dad's funeral.

"We'd like a short service, please," said Mum.

"Three hymns, a reading and a prayer. And some music while people are coming in."

"And tell me what you'd like me to say about Pete," said the minister.

Pete was Dad's name. Steve didn't want to hear that bit. He helped Gemma choose one of the hymns. Then he went out into the garden.

It was getting dark. He sat on the swing and for the umpteenth time he wished he had a cat. A soft, furry body to sit on his lap and purr while he stroked it.

They couldn't have a cat because Dad was allergic to them.

Steve's thoughts stopped with a jerk. Dad wasn't here any more. There was no reason now not to have a cat. Only he couldn't possibly ask for one at the moment. Maybe one day.

He heard the minister leaving. He went indoors and turned on the television. It was a cowboy film. Steve watched it without really noticing what was going on, until a man got killed. A woman in the film rushed up to him. She cradled him in her arms and wept. And Steve began to cry. Ever since Dad died he hadn't cried at all. Now he was crying as if he would never stop.

Gemma found him. She was frightened.

"Mum!" she called. "Quick!"

Mum came rushing in. She gathered Steve to her and rocked him gently.

"Cry, darling, cry," she whispered. "Let it all come out."

Gemma stood watching. Tears began to roll down her face. It was quite a while before they all felt better.

"Another cup of tea," said Mum as Steve wiped his eyes and blew his nose. "Then we'll think of something nice to do."

Five

They played hide and seek all round the house. It was fun.

On the Sunday they went for a long walk. In the evening Steve and Gemma each wrote a letter to Dad. They put in all the things they wanted to say to him, and said goodbye.

The letters were to be put on the coffin with the flowers at the funeral. They were another one of the things that were sad to do but made them feel better afterwards.

Like parcelling up Dad's things for the charity shop. Mum gave Steve Dad's watch, and Gemma his travelling clock. She kept his camera, and a few other things. Steve sneaked a pair of Dad's gloves. Something warm and soft to touch.

All the friends and relations had to be invited to the funeral.

"Last one. Awful Aunt Hetty!" said Mum, picking up the phone yet again.

"Mum!" Steve and Gemma were horror-struck. "You're not inviting her!"

"I must," said Mum. "She is your dad's aunt. And since she lives on that remote Scottish island of hers we shall have to invite her to stay for at least two nights."

Steve and Gemma pretended to be sick.

Mum tried to look on the bright side. "We could be all right. It depends on her latest craze."

Aunt Hetty had had a craze for singing in her loud, untuneful voice. She'd had a craze for striped clothes, and had brought them some which they'd all had to wear during that visit. Then she'd had a craze for craft work, and they'd all had to get extremely messy making unlikely objects.

"Maybe she's taken up reading," suggested Mum. "We'll soon know."

The funeral was to be on Thursday morning. Aunt Hetty was invited for Wednesday. Because of her long journey she didn't arrive till they were home from school.

They heard the taxi drive up. All three of them rushed to peep out of the window.

"She's dyed her hair bright ginger!" giggled Gemma. "She looks like a lollipop!"

"She's certainly still as thin as a stick," said Mum. Aunt Hetty finished paying the taxi driver, and stood tapping her foot while he unwillingly unloaded her suitcase from the back.

"She's only staying two nights," grumbled Steve. "Why does she need that huge case?"

They soon found out. When the greetings were over Steve helped to lug the case upstairs. Inside, nestling among aunt Hetty's underwear were two dumb-bells. Steve and Gemma watched, fascinated, as Aunt

Hetty unpacked them. Her present craze was Super Fitness.

She gave Gemma a hard look. "You've got fatter, dear. You must join me when I get down to my Programme."

"Programme?" asked Gemma, hating Aunt Hetty for saying she'd got fatter.

"My Super Fitness Programme." Steve could tell Aunt Hetty was giving each word a capital letter.

Now she was looking at him.

"You must join in too, Steven," she announced. "Exercise is good for everyone. Especially in - " she stopped, then finished in a whisper "- times like these."

Steve felt furious. He wanted to say, "What times, Aunt Hetty? Times like when your dad's just been killed?"

Instead he turned on his heel and walked out of the room. His face was burning. He didn't know where to go or what to do. He wanted Dad.

"Steve!" Mum called from the kitchen. "Could you come and help me?"

He went downstairs. Mum could see he was upset; but she didn't say anything, just gave his hair a quick ruffle.

He set to work peeling potatoes, fixing his mind on the thickness of the potato skins and nothing else.

The potatoes were wasted on Aunt Hetty, who refused to eat them.

Exactly one hour after the meal she carried out

some of her Programme, pounding up and down the stairs in a skimpy leotard, her bony arms and legs waving wildly.

She looks like a mad stick insect, thought Steve. He couldn't wait to see her with the dumb-bells.

They all went upstairs for a demonstration.

Aunt Hetty could just about lift them off the ground before she had to let them drop. It was all Mum and Steve could do not to laugh out loud. Gemma had to go behind the dressing table and stuff paper hankies into her mouth.

Mum got Aunt Hetty's mind off Super Fitness by asking if she wanted to phone the relatives who lived locally. Aunt Hetty seized the chance. Steve and Gemma seized the dumb-bells. By the time Aunt Hetty had finished talking, the dumb-bells were safely put away in her case and it was bedtime.

Next morning was cold and grey. Even Aunt Hetty was quiet at breakfast. After breakfast there was food to get ready for when they came back from the funeral.

Steve noticed the pile of letters and cards of sympathy on the hall table. They'd been arriving every day since Dad died. Steve had only glanced at them. Gemma didn't want to see them at all.

People soon started arriving. Grandparents, aunts, uncles, cousins, friends. The sitting room was overcrowded with people, all looking posher than usual. Except for Uncle Bob they all spoke in low voices.

Steve hated it. He was even grateful Aunt Hetty was there to answer the door.

It was a relief when the undertaker came to tell them it was time. They all filed out of the house.

There was quite a procession on the way to the church. First the big black hearse carrying the coffin and the beautiful flowers, with Steve's and Gemma's letters. Then the limousines for Mum, Uncle Bob, Steve and Gemma, with another for the grandparents. Then a line of ordinary cars for everyone else.

They reached the church. It was hard following Dad's coffin down the aisle. Steve was glad the service was short. He tried not to notice Mum's tears.

No one could have missed Aunt Hetty crying. Loud sobs. Huge nose blowing. Steve looked at Gemma. They couldn't help grinning. The service ended. The organ played. The funeral attendants lifted the coffin. Everyone followed it out into the churchyard. Steve hated the moment when the coffin was lowered into the ground. He held Gemma's hand. She squeezed his hand tight.

But the minister said some very comforting words about seeing each other again some day.

It was over. Everyone was moving away, and Mum was thanking people for coming, and telling them they were welcome back at the house.

I hope they don't all come, thought Steve.

Six

Back at the house Grandad whisked the children upstairs. He had a present for each of them hidden in Mum's room.

They unwrapped them. Gemma had a chemistry set she'd wanted for a long time. Steve had a video game.

"Thank you, Grandad!" they said, giving him a hug.

Thinking about the presents helped them to be polite to all the visitors, who were now eating sandwiches and drinking tea or coffee. Aunt Hetty, still in her black clothes, was demonstrating the up and downstairs part of her Programme.

This time she looks like a demented spider, thought Steve. Everyone except Aunt Hetty was trying not to laugh. They were all talking in their usual voices now, even the grandparents.

All of a sudden Steve missed Dad. No one here really cares, he thought angrily. He found his metal detector and went out into the garden. He put on the earphones and switched it on, sweeping the detector backwards and forwards just above the ground.

Someone touched him on the shoulder. Steve jumped. He looked round. It was Uncle Bob. Reluctantly Steve switched off the detector.

"Found anything?" asked Uncle Bob.

Steve shook his head. "Not today." He swallowed hard.

"Sandwich?" Uncle Bob held one out. Steve shook his head.

"Steve," Uncle Bob said, "I promise you it won't always hurt so much. And I know it's not the same as having your dad, but if you or Gemma want anything - or want to talk about anything, any time - well, I'm here."

Steve nodded.

"Come on." Uncle Bob was halfway to the gate. "Forget the sandwich.. Put your metal detector in the porch. Let's sneak out and get ourselves some chips."

Steve hesitated. Chips were his favourite food. Besides, all the friends and relations would be shocked.

He made up his mind. "OK."

They bent low as they passed the open windows of the sitting room. Uncle Bob tripped and nearly went sprawling into a bush. Steve giggled. Uncle Bob's shoulders began to shake. Shushing each other, they could hardly hold in their laughter.

Uncle Bob reached the pavement and started to race down the road. Steve went racing after him. It turned out to be the best bit of the day.

Very early in the morning Aunt Hetty left. They were all glad to see her and her dumb-bells leaving. But somehow things were worse when she'd gone. They didn't have to try to be polite in front of guests any more. Gemma shouted at Mum. Mum shouted at Gemma. They had a full-blown row. All the way to school nobody spoke.

Mum and Steve said goodbye to each other as usual, but Gemma still wouldn't speak. Steve looked anxiously at Mum.

"You're a rotten pig!" he told Gemma as they went up the school path. It didn't help. Gemma kicked out at him and ran away.

Suppose something happened to Mum. People had accidents when they were upset. Perhaps she'd have an accident on the way home. Or when she got home. Anything might happen to her.

He worried all day. Every time the classroom door opened he thought it would be a message for him to go the head.

No message came. At home time Mum was there at the school gate as usual. Steve could hardly speak for relief. Gemma came bouncing down the path, chattering away. Mum was talking too, telling them about her day.

Steve had another awful thought. Perhaps they'd have an accident now, on the way home...

They didn't. There were no more accidents. Only the three of them getting angry quicker than usual. He and Gemma fighting more than usual.

It was strange without Dad. No Dad coming in after work. No Dad calming them all down. No Dad sitting in his chair with the paper. No Dad at meal times.

It's worse for Mum, thought Steve. I ought to look after her.

He started to ask if he could go shopping for her. Take her breakfast in bed. Do the housework for her.

Mainly she didn't let him.

Steve grew more and more anxious. He tried to make Gemma behave properly. That only meant more rows.

He thought about asking Uncle Bob to help. But taking care of Mum was Steve's job, and he wasn't managing it . . .

One afternoon he blew up, shouting at everyone.

They'd just got in from school. Gemma wouldn't let him choose the programme on the television, and it all got too much.

Mum and Gemma looked at him in shocked silence. Then Mum took him into the kitchen, sat him on a chair facing her, and said firmly, "Steve, this has got to stop!"

Steve looked at her in surprise.

"Darling," she said, "stop worrying about me! You don't have to! I'm fine, and I'm going to be even better. Of course we all miss Dad. That's why we all look after each other. Families do that. It's not a job for one person on his own." She smiled at him.

Steve felt as if a tremendous weight had gone.

"Are you sure?" he asked.

"Absolutely certain," she said. "Truly truly wooly pooly."

He grinned. They'd always said that silly rhyme. It was a family thing. They were still a family.

Mum back at work, school going on, his club meetings . . . Some people seemed to think Steve's life was right back to normal.

They were wrong. It wasn't.

Seven

Without Dad Steve felt as if his whole world had changed. He wasn't doing as well at school. He couldn't seem to listen to the teachers, or care about how he did the work. Some of the teachers were kind. Some of them weren't.

Gemma was always in trouble these days. She kept losing her temper. Yet sometimes she was really nice to Steve.

Steve knew things could have been worse. They had enough money at home, what with Mum's job and the insurance money from Dad's accident. They kept the house, and he and Gemma stayed at the same school.

"It takes time, pet," Mrs Vickers said to him one day when he was gloomily helping her peg huge piles of washing on the line. "It's a big thing to get used to. Don't you fret."

He was glad to go to his club meetings. Final plans were being made for the camp at Jukes' Farm. They were going to sleep in their sleeping bags in the barn. Mrs Soames was coming as general helper and first aid person.

Mr Soames told them about the metal detecting they would do. The farm had been there for absolutely ages, and there was a big chance of finding money that people had dropped in olden times. There was also a story that treasure had once been buried there, to hide it from the Roundheads. No one had found it. So far.

"I bet we find it!" said Jim and Steve.

"No harm in dreaming," chuckled Mr Soames. "I'm afraid we're more likely to find coins, buckles and buttons. That's exciting enough, when you think who might have lost them, and how long ago it was."

"Anyway, everyone" - he raised his voice - "remember you do have to have permission to use metal detectors these days. We're very grateful to Farmer Jukes for allowing us on his farm. We might want him to invite us again. So we'll behave ourselves. Right?"

"Right, Mr Soames," chorused the club members. When he got home from the meeting, Steve said, "Mum, could I borrow Dad's camera for the trip? Dad used to let me use it."

"I know he did," Mum said. "And yes you can."

"Thanks, Mum!" Steve's face glowed. Then he hesitated. "Mum - is it OK to talk about Dad?"

"Of course it is!" Mum was amazed. "We don't want to pretend he was never here! Let's get the camera now, and look at some of the old photographs."

Gemma came in. The three of them sat on Mum's bed looking at photographs, laughing at the funny ones.

"Happy days," sighed Mum. Then she shook herself. "And lots more happy days to come. Now - can you afford the film, Steve?"

"Easily", said Steve. He had a lot of pocket money saved up.

Slowly he began to do better at school. Gemma began to settle down too. They were getting used to life without Dad, although things that hurt still turned up unexpectedly. Things like hearing Dad's favourite tune, or seeing someone else's dad.

At last it was Wednesday of half term. Mum and Gemma took Steve to the club hall just after lunch and saw him on to the minibus with everyone else. He sat next to Jim and waved from the window.

I hope they'll be all right, he thought anxiously. But next minute Jim was offering him one of his famous sticky toffees, the minibus started, and they were off.

It was getting dark by the time they arrived at the farm. Steve could just make out the farmhouse - white walled, lattice-windowed, with a porch over its front door. He was a bit disappointed it didn't still have its thatched roof; but it did have honeysuckle climbing up over the porch, even if there were no flowers growing on it at the moment.

Farmer Jukes came out to greet them. He led them round to the back door and into the kitchen, with its flagstoned floor and oak-beamed ceiling. Fortunately the kitchen was large enough for the whole party to squeeze in at once. They settled hungrily round the huge table.

Mrs Jukes had a meal ready - farmhouse stew,

followed by baked apples and custard. It was delicious. Steve had been sharing his chair with a large, fat tabby cat. Now Mrs Jukes had time to notice.

"That's Tiddles," she smiled. "Push her off if you want to, dear. We're spoiling her a bit at the moment. She's due to have her kittens any minute now."

"She's all right," Steve said. He loved to have her there. He stroked her, and she purred.

"Come on, detectors!" Mr Soames rallied everyone. "We've got to set up camp!"

A space had been cleared for them in the barn. They put down big plastic sheets and laid the sleeping bags on top of them. The metal detectors and special spades were arranged neatly in a row.
When everything was done they dived over to the farmhouse bathrooms, then back to the barn. There was a lot of fun as they got ready for bed.

Presently they were all settled. Mr Soames told them stories of metal detecting. In spite of the strangeness, and the hard floor, Steve felt himself drifting into sleep. His last thought was of treasure to find tomorrow.

Eight

Thursday was a bit disappointing for Steve and Jim.
They worked for almost two hours in the morning, and
didn't find a thing. Their arms ached, their backs ached
and their necks ached, although they tried to remember
about keeping as upright as possible.

The club had a break at lunch time, with meat
pies, fruit and juice. Then Mrs Soames took them for a
Nature walk.

There was time for another short go at metal
detecting before the evening meal. This time Jim heard
what Mr Soames called 'flak', a sort of clicking, on his
metal detector. Excitedly, Steve handed Jim the special
spade. Jim dug down, while everyone came to watch.
It was an old iron nail.

"Better than nothing," said Mr Soames cheerily.
Jim nodded. As a matter of fact he was very pleased
with his nail, although it would have been better if it had
been treasure. He replaced the earth carefully, and the
search went on.

Mrs Jukes called them in for the evening meal
sausages, mash and beans, followed by jam roly-poly.

Steve looked round for Tiddles. Mrs Jukes shook
her head.

"I don't know where she's gone. I'm right

worried about her. She went out last night and I haven't
seen her since. She'll have had those kittens somewhere,
that's for sure. She always hides away to have them.
But she comes in for her own food."

"Would you like us to search round?" asked Mr
Soames. "That I would!" said Mrs Jukes.

It was getting dark before the meal was over.
They all searched, calling "Tiddles! Tiddles!"

It was no use.

"There are so many places to hide on a farm,"
sighed Mrs Jukes. "Sheds, woodpiles, nooks and
crannies..."

"I'm sure she'll turn up," comforted Mrs Soames.

During the night a storm blew up. The other boys
slept right through it, but it woke Steve. He lay listening
to the howling wind, and the lashing rain. He couldn't
help worrying about Tiddles. Suppose she wasn't
somewhere safe? Suppose she'd got trapped, or injured?
And what about the kittens? He knew why Mrs Jukes
had looked so upset.

He dozed off again at last. When he woke the
sun was shining through cracks in the barn door, but
everyone else still seemed to be asleep.

Steve climbed out of his bag and tiptoed across
the floor.

"Mr Soames!" he whispered.

Mr Soames peered up at him sleepily. "Steve?"

"Can I get up and go over to the farmhouse?"
Steve asked. "I want to see if Tiddles has come back."

"What?" Mr Soames looked astonished. Then he said, "All right, but be careful."

Steve dressed quickly and silently, and got his metal detector. Two minutes later he was in the farm kitchen, having stopped for a dash into the toilet on his way

Farmer Jukes was already out working in the fields. Mrs Jukes looked quite upset.

"No, Tiddles isn't back," she told Steve.

"I've had an idea!" Steve's eyes shone eagerly. "Tiddles is wearing a collar, isn't she! With a name tag on!"

"Ay. A brass name tag," Mrs Jukes agreed.

Rapidly Steve told her the story of the shepherd finding the sheep in the snow, Mrs Jukes shook her head.

"It's good of you, pet, but I don't think metal detecting will help this time."

"I want to try!" said Steve. He ran outside to the outbuildings. Quickly he swept over the floors with his detector.

One or two false alarms. No cat.

The club was up and about now, coming in to wash, thinking about breakfast. Steve didn't want to stop. He didn't want to talk. He had to find Tiddles. The old shed, down near the pasture. He'd had a specially good search round it last night. But maybe Tiddles hadn't wanted to be found last night. Maybe she'd been hiding. Or in the middle of having her kittens...

He ran down the rutted track.

Suddenly he realised something he hadn't properly noticed the night before. Sometime yesterday there'd been a delivery of drainage pipes. They were stacked along one side of the shed.

He knew the shed was raised a bit off the ground. It had a wooden floor which was up on bricks. If there was a gap in the bricks, big enough for a cat to get through, and if the gap was the side where the pipes were now, maybe Tiddles had been under the floor and got trapped. She would have crouched, hiding, afraid of the noise when the pipes were delivered.

Steve tried to peer under them, but he couldn't be sure whether there was a gap or not. Mr Jukes wouldn't want to move the pipes in case Tiddles was trapped. Besides, he'd have to get extra men to help.

"Puss! Puss!" he called. "Tiddles!"

There was a meow! Then another, louder!

"Tiddles! Hang on!" cried Steve.

Clutching his metal detector he raced back up the track, into the farmhouse.

The others had just started breakfast without him.

"I've found her!" he cried. "At least," he added more quietly, "I think I have."

"Where?" Mrs Jukes nearly dropped the cup she'd been holding.

"Under the shed!" Steve was almost too breathless to speak, but he led the rush back to the shed.

They were all panting by the time they got there.

"Tiddles! Tiddles!" called Mrs Jukes.

Nothing. Not a sound. Steve felt awful.

"I did hear a meow!" he insisted. "I did!"

"Maybe she's too frightened to meow with us all here, pet," said Mrs Jukes.

"Or maybe you imagined it," said Mr Soames. He wasn't at his best in the morning.

Then Steve remembered his metal detector.

"Wait!" he said. Carefully he opened the creaky door. He switched on the detector and began to sweep it across the floor. Nothing. Nothing. Then - Beep beep! Beep beep!

"There!" he cried. "It's picking up Tiddles' metal tag!"

"Or nails," said Mr Soames.

Steve bit his lip. He knew he was right.

"Try it again, pet," said Mrs Jukes.

Steve tried again, over exactly the same spot. Nothing.

"There," said Mr Soames.

"Wait!" Steve tried again, a little further over. Beep beep! Beep beep! "It is her!" he cried. "She's moving, under the floor! That's why the sound moved!"

"I believe you're right!" cried Mr Soames.

"Stand back, everyone!" commanded Mrs Jukes. "I'm not waiting for Mr Jukes! I'm getting this floor up!"

She knelt, and began to pull up the rotting

floorboards with her bare hands.

Next moment she gave a cry, pulled out a very dusty dishevelled Tiddles, and shouted, "She's had them! Four kittens!"

Everyone got even more excited. They all wanted to crowd into the shed and peer under the floor.

In the end Mr and Mrs Soames got the club members to come away by reminding them of breakfast.

Steve was allowed to stay. He picked up the four tiny, helpless creatures and put them in his pockets while Mrs Jukes held a strongly protesting Tiddles.

The kittens and cat were settled in a basket in an upstairs room. Tiddles was given food and a litter tray.

"And she's not going outside for a while!" smiled Mrs Jukes. "I'm not having her moving those kittens out again! Wait till Mr Jukes hears about this! Thank you, Steve pet. I can't thank you enough!"

Steve felt great. He had breakfast alone with Mrs Jukes. Even Jim had gone off with the club. Steve didn't care.

After breakfast he asked if he could take a photograph of Tiddles and the kittens. Mrs Jukes said yes. She knew he'd be careful not to frighten them.

Steve fetched the camera and quietly opened the door to the upstairs room. Tiddles and her kittens were cuddled up together. Steve took the photograph. He hoped it was a good one. I'll be able to show Dad, he thought.

Memory stabbed him. He couldn't show Dad. Dad was dead.

The tears started. Steve struggled to brush them away. Tiddles had been washing a kitten. Now she stopped. She looked up at him. It was as if she knew he was upset.

"Cats know a lot," Steve told her.

He looked at the tiny kittens. There's dying, and there's being born, he thought. It's all part of life going on. My life is going on too . . .

He'd need to take more photographs as the kittens grew. Maybe he'd be able to have one of the kittens when they were old enough.

He glanced out of the window. The club was in the next field. Their metal detectors were sweeping the ground.

Steve took one last look at Tiddles. Then he hurried out of the room, closed the door carefully, and rushed down to get his metal detector.

Maybe this was the day. The day he found buried treasure!

Organisations

Cruse/Bereavement Care
Headquarters
Cruse House
126 Sheen Road
Richmond, Surrey
TW9 1UR
Tel: 0181 940 4818
Helpline: 0181 332 7227
Information and advice on bereavement.

Childline
Freepost 1111
London N1 0BR
Tel: 0800 1111
*24-hour, free and confidential advice line
to help children with a wide range of
issues. They will listen, comfort and
protect.*

The Samaritans
46 Marshall Street
London W1
Tel: 0171 734 2800
*Local branches are listed on the inside
back or inside front cover of the
telephone directory. They give emotional
support and are confidential and non-
judgmental.*

AUSTRALIA
Kids Help Line (free)
Tel: 008 073 008
Salvo Youth Line (free)
Tel: 1800 251 008

NEW ZEALAND
Youthline
PO Box 9300
Newmarket, Auckland
Tel: 09 376 6633

SOUTH AFRICA
Child Emergency Service
Tel: 08001 23321
*Free 24-hour service. They give advice
on a wide range of subjects and can refer
you to other relevant organisations.*

Books

The following are all available from Cruse/Bereavement Care (address and telephone number given on page 47).

HELP FOR BEREAVED CHILDREN

Caring for Bereaved Children
Children feel grief but may show it differently from adults. This useful booklet by a Cruse counsellor enables parents, relatives, teachers and others to understand the child's grief, and suggests ways of helping.

FICTION FOR CHILDREN

John's Book by Jill Fuller
for 7- to 11-year-olds
John is 10 when his father dies suddenly. He goes through a turbulent period before learning to trust life again. Illustrated.

Comfort Herself by G Kaye
For 11-year-olds upwards
Bereavement often involves children in change and decisions. The story of a girl who, after her English mother dies in a car crash, goes to Ghana to join her Ghanian father.

OTHER BOOKS

Let's Talk About Death and Dying by Pete Sanders (Franklin Watts)
Let's Talk About looks at subjects of specific interest to young children and asks and answers the question they most frequently raise. The series covers issues which affect children's lives or which add to their growing awareness of the world. Simple clear texts are illustrated with colourful photographs.